I0765525

The BIG Journey Project

The BIG Journey Project shows young readers how one girl finds inspiration through a class project and working collaboratively with her friends. As they embark to discover the true meaning of diversity and inclusion, this heartwarming story embraces differences that exists in many communities with ethnically diverse families and various cultural traditions.

This book encourages young children to explore and recognize that we all have differences and we all have something in common if we look hard enough.

Dianna is on a big journey to find out what diversity and inclusion is really all about and why this is such a big topic every day. Dianna's cape taps into her supershero mission of Ubuntu!

Join Dianna and her classmates on this wonderful adventure of discovery where she learns what is really important related to diversity and inclusion.

Don't forget your cape.

DEDICATION

This book is dedicated to all of the young children who continue to take the BIG journey as good-natured, courageous, determined, insightful, motivated, daring, and epic hero's.

Dream on. Dream BIG.
Make a Difference!

Published by Purpose Publishing
1503 Main Street #168, Grandview, MO 64030
www.PurposePublishing.com

The BIG Journey Project

Illustrations and Cover design by: Natasha Beauchamp

Printed in the United States of America

Inquiries may be addressed to:
www.DrAndreaHendricks.com
Email: asdr1364@sbcglobal.net

This book is available in quantity discounts for bulk purchases.
For more information contact www.DrAndreaHendricks.com

The BIG Journey Project
BOLD INCLUSION FOR GREATNESS
BUTTER EFF
5G & ROBOTT
MEDICINE
Story by: DR. ANDREA HENDRICKS
with Illustrations by: Natasha Beauchamp

"Let's talk Diversity! Who knows what that is?" Mrs. Boyd looked around the class. No one responded. Dianna bit her lip. "Intersectionality? Anyone?" Mrs. Boyd inquired aloud.

Jordan raised his hand, "Is... is it something to do with cross-roads...?"
"Go on." insisted Mrs. Boyd.
"Um, well. Intersections are where roads meet up...?" Jordan said hesitantly.

"Good! Yes, intersectionality is all about meeting up, but meeting up with leveraging differences rather than roads." Everyone looked confused. Mrs. Boyd smiled. "Back to diversity?"

Dianna raised her hand. "Is it something to do with differences too? Like being Muslim or black or a girl?"

"Yes! What does diversity mean when it comes to differences though?" asked Mrs. Boyd.

"Does it mean differences are allowed? I mean, like a lady can be a janitor or a man can be a nurse? That sort of thing?" asked T.J.

"Yes, exactly!", Mrs. Boyd replied. "Diversity and inclusion are all about embracing differences and making it so that everyone can do what they want to do."

"For real!" said Jordan as he moved his wheelchair back a bit, "I want to play NBA basketball. Nothing can make that happen!"

"Actually..." T.J., a tall boy sitting at the table, spoke up, "There's wheelchair basketball now. They're really good, they play hard and fast. You should try it, Jord."

"Maybe..." said Jordan, looking thoughtfully.

"Anyway," said Mrs. Boyd. "There is a worksheet with all the information about the last award of the year. I want everyone to do some activities and write a project about them for the annual fair, next month. It should be on your tablets."

Dianna waved goodbye as the bell rang.

Dianna ran out, waving to her mom who was waiting with Maria, her little sister, and Anthony, her big brother. "Hi Mom. Hi guys!" said Dianna.

Maria said "Hi!" back, but Anthony just glanced up from his phone for a minute. Dianna hopped into the car and buckled up. "So, what's new?" Mom asked.

"Mrs. Boyd emailed us the worksheet for the last award!" Dianna said with excitement. Dianna already had all the other prizes and this one would make it the full set.

They drove out of the school, waving at T.J. who was riding his bike home. He waved back as they drove past him. As they drove along, Dianna took out her tablet, clicked it on and said. "Oh no!"

"What? What's the matter?" Her mother asked. "This is... hard!" Diana responded.
"The assignment? We'll look at it at home - put it away for now." Mom said.

Dianna did as her mother said, feeling puzzled and wondering how she could get the award for this. This will be the biggest assignment she'd ever done.

I
AM
BEAUTIFUL
Certificate
SuperShero
Diana

At home, they went to Dianna's beautiful bedroom. It was pink, green, and plush and Dianna loved every inch of it!

They looked at the tablet together, watched over by glittery pictures on the wall, and a pair of curious goldfish who lived on Dianna's pink and green princess desk. In front of her desk was a corkboard on which Dianna had proudly pinned her certificates for all the other awards she had won.

For the last learning award she needed to show that she understood:
Intersectionality
Diversity
Inclusion

But how? she thought. She didn't understand them at all!
Suddenly, she felt something go around her shoulders. It was her cape!
Mom rested her hands on Dianna's shoulders.

"You can do this Dianna. You're a supershero!" said mom. "But for now, go play with your brother and sister while I make dinner."

"Okay!" Dianna said as she swirled her cape around her shoulders and bounced out of her bedroom. She headed to the big tree at the bottom of the large garden.

The tree was her favorite place to think, and she was still puzzled about her assignment. Dianna knew that sitting by her tree, wearing her cape, made her feel special and strong like she could do anything.

Dianna remembers a story her grandmother shared about her ancestors.
She started writing in her journal.

All of a sudden, Maria and Anthony waved for her to join them, and the three of them raced around the big garden until their mother called them in for dinner.

While they ate, Dianna asked, "What is intersectionality?"
Dianna's dad smiled and said, "That's what you have to find out!"

Her mom said, "It means being aware that people have different needs and providing for them. Taking all their differences into account." Dianna frowned.

"For example... Dianna's mom said aloud as she thought for a minute, 'Jordan has physical limitations, right?' They all nodded. "So, he can't get around the school easily like you, right?" They agreed.

"So, the school has ramps and other accommodations so that Jordan and others can participate in all classes and events like you." Mom explained.

"Oh!" said Dianna as she thought for a minute, "So, it's like knowing that not everyone is the same?" "Yes, exactly. But it's much more than physical things that intersectionality takes into account. We all have multiple dimensions to our lives too." Mom continued.

"Like what?" asked Dianna.
"Dimensions that are visible or invisible to others – like gender, age, race, culture, etc...."

"How?" asked Dianna.
"Sometimes the solution is very simple once you just start thinking from other people's points of view." Mom continued to explain as she started cutting the pie at the dinner table. "Intersectionality is ensuring that programs and services are interlocking and interwoven throughout the school—allowing students to bring their whole self to class."

"It focuses on the question 'does the person matter'—'are they allowed to bring their whole self to school?" Mom finished.

Dianna had a lot to think about. After dinner, she changed into her pajamas, put on her cape, went back outside and sat under the big tree to get started with the assignment.

She would scribble down an idea, but then shake her head. She crumpled up the paper and threw it down.

She was nearly in tears when it suddenly came to her. She had a plan! She stood up, stretched, and took a moment to gather up all of the ideas before phoning T.J.

"Hi, T.J.—I have an idea." Then, she phoned Jordan and told him the same thing.

The next day, they all met in Dianna's backyard under the tree—it was her thinking place.

Jordan's wheelchair bumped over the lawn and he looked up into the tree with a wishful expression on his face, he smiled. "I sure miss climbing", he said. "Anyway. What did you want to talk about, Dianna?" She explained her idea and waited to see what they thought.

T.J. said, "I love it!!!" And Jordan said, "I love it too!!! Let's get started."

Dianna, with her cape on, clapped her hands and said "Okay, let's get started." Jordan and T.J. exchanged a look. "Why do you wear that cape?" asked T.J.

"Oh, the cape inspires me. I love supersheroes!" said Dianna "Don't you mean superheroes?", asked Jordan.

Dianna—put her hands on her hip and said "No—I am a girl and I am a supershero, just like Vice President, Kamala Harris. She wore a purple suit too." "Got it! Where do we start? asked T.J.

The next day, they all went to town to meet their grandmothers at a local Mexican restaurant. The grandmothers would see if they could find some things to help their grandchildren understand diversity, inclusion, and intersectionality.

They saw Jordan's Granny Nora first. She was walking up the street wearing her Riverdance clothes and carrying her shopping bag. She just left her favorite cultural dance session at the community center and picked up a few items from the farmers market. The children offered to help her, but she said, "I may be older than you, but I'm not that old yet! I can manage, thank you kindly!" Dianna laughed. She was looking forward to the conversation.

Next, they saw T.J.'s Abuela Tina through the restaurant window dancing to great music with her friends.

They went into the restaurant and Dianna spoke to Abuela Tina for a minute and then they all sat down at the table.   T.J.'s grandmother made everyone feel welcomed. The hostess gave T.J., Jordan, and Dianna sombreros to wear. Abuela Tina loves to dance and shared that her family comes to this restaurant for many years. "It is a great tradition to connect with family and friends over music and food." said Abuela Tina.

Grandma Mae just finished choir practice at their local church. Dianna's grandmother loved to wear beautiful church hats. Now, all their grandmothers were sitting together! The three ladies were good friends and were eager to help their grandchildren. While they ate great traditional Mexican food, they shared stories of the old days and made plans to lend the children special items to show and tell at the fair. After dinner, they danced a while and then went their separate ways. T.J., Jordan, and Dianna were spending the weekend with their grandmothers to gather more details about diversity.

T.J.'s Abuela's house was a very spiritual setting.   It was beautifully decorated.   Their family life revolved around frequent rituals, ceremonies, and celebrations. Abuela Tina enjoyed hosting family gatherings.   She shared, "Our family ties are strong in Mexican culture and have been for centuries. Our families will always be rooted in tradition." said Abuela Tina as she pulled a box out from the hallway closet.

"Two of the best-known pieces of Mexican traditions are the Sombrero hat, like the one you and your friends wore tonight and the pointy boots.   Your grandfather and his father wore them.   They are often called Tribal boots.   Mexican men wear pointy boots for traditional events and parties."

"We love to dance in our family. Right now, I am so tired from dancing tonight.   Buena noches mi amor" said Abuela Tina.   She gave T.J. a box with more items to showcase at the annual fair.

At the kitchen table, Jordan and his Granny Nora shared stories of the Irish cultural traditions.He learned that two of the top Irish traditions are spending time with family and dancing. Granny Nora shared that dancing is an age-old art form and has been in our culture like Riverdance for many years. Jordan remembers his family loves to attend the annual Riverdance festival.

He enjoyed seeing his grandparent's combine Irish stepdance and Ceili dancing into their unique forms and fashions. Granny Nora went to bed. Jordan was looking forward to seeing his Granny dance in the upcoming Riverdance festival. He now knew the importance of that cultural event.

At Dianna's grandmother's house, she sipped hot chocolate and prepared for bed. Grandma Mae shared one of her favorite books called Ubuntu and a photo album.

"Ubuntu is the ability to honor humanity through compassion—humanity to others. I am what I am because of who we all are to others. 'Dianna, I know you like trees.' The tree on the cover of this book is a guiding symbol of diversity for many cultures—especially the African culture. The tree symbolizes the roots of who you are and brings focus to how the work in diversity and inclusion branches out and flourishes overtime to connect to who you are."

Grandma Mae continued, "The tree teaches us important lessons about responsibility, power, and legacy. The tree creates an inclusive interaction between generations, including generations that aren't even born yet. Dianna found the book to be inspiring. Her grandmother said, "Dianna your quest in life is figuring out who you are, an important part of this journey—to connect to your culture and heritage".

"Until you discover where you come from, you will not be able to fully appreciate where you are going or your purpose and power." Her grandmother gave her a box. "Goodnight Dianna—sweet dreams." said Grandma Mae. As Dianna fell asleep, she could not wait to share the great things she learned with T.J. and Jordan. She knew they had great stories from their culture as well.

It was the day of the fair. Dianna started setting up the display. She was wearing her Grandma Mae's kanga (a traditional African dress) with a broad, flat necklace that her mom had carefully fastened around her neck. T.J. looked confident in his bright clothing and wide-brimmed sombrero and pointy boots. When he saw Dianna, he grinned and gave her a double thumbs-up, and relaxed, flapping his poncho as he walked over.

Jordan whistled as he rolled through the open door. 'You guys look great!' he exclaimed. 'Wow, thank you!' giggled Dianna, twirling to show him how the dress flared out as she spun. 'What are you wearing, Jord?' He indicated the green floppy cap, a tam-o'-shanter, on his head and the kilt that came down to his knees. 'Yo, that's a kilt. Isn't that Scottish?' T.J. was curious.

Jordan shook his head, 'No', kilts can be Scottish, but we, Irish, wore them too. 'Wow, that's cool!' T.J. The bell rang to signal the beginning of the annual fair. Dianna and T.J. stood behind the table, while Jordan wheeled into his place between them. They were ready to share their BIG Journey.

BIG DIVERSITY
PROJECT
INTERSECTIONALITY: MULTIPLE DIMENSIONS OF
DIVERSITY
INCLUSION: MAKING SPACE FOR OTHERS TO SHINE
DIVERSE IDEAS: ALLOWING OTHERS TO SHARE THEIR
STORIES
DIVERSE INTERACTIONS: LISTENING TO THE PAST AND
PRESENT. GENERATIONAL DIVERSITY (THEIR
GRANDMOTHERS/COMMUNITY).
INNOVATION: MULTIPLE WAYS TO SHOWCASE THE
PROJECT
BUTTER
EFFE
MEDICINE
5G
ROBOTT
ART
EALS
JUDGE
JUDGE
JUDGE
JUDGE

The judges and Mrs. Boyd walked to each table in turn. When she came to Dianna's, she was surprised. 'Boys?' 'We teamed up to make a BIG impact on this project, Mrs. Boyd!' 'OK, then, show me.' replied Mrs. Boyd.

Dianna explained that she invited Jordan and T. J. to help with the project. By pooling time, with their experiences, they had all created a better project than any one of them could have done. Then, she pressed 'play' on their video presentation which detailed their BIG diversity journey through their communities, meeting with grandmothers and collecting diverse items displayed on the table—-where they came from and why they were important.

At the conclusion—Dianna said "A person is a person through other people. I cannot exist until I see you, honor you, and see your strengths."

Our BIG Journey honored that no matter what culture— we love family, music, dancing, and great food.

The judges and Mrs. Boyd's took notes on Dianna's team:
Intersectionality: multiple dimensions of diversity.
Inclusion: making space for others to shine.
Diverse ideas: allowing others to share their stories.
Diverse interactions: listening to the past and present.
Generational diversity (their grandmothers/community).
Innovation: multiple ways to showcase the project.

Mrs. Boyd went to the podium.   All teams were assembled on stage ready to hear the final announcement. Mrs. Boyd shared, "The team recognized today would be a team that thought about how to include others, make allowances for differences – how to make a space where everyone feels welcomed and free to leverage strengths. And most of all, demonstrated how to leverage, experience, develop and cultivate diversity, inclusion, and intersectionality across cultures for the greater good."

Mrs. Boyd said, "The winners are... Dianna, T.J., and Jordan.   They understand that diversity is rich and diversity is the value add at school and in the community." The room erupted in big applause.

Dianna pulled her cape out of her bag and swung it over her kanga. She wrapped it around her shoulders as they went to the podium to get the trophy from Mrs. Boyd. She felt happier than she ever had before.

T.J. and Jordan had a big smile on their faces.

Her family was standing near the stage, clapping the loudest of all. Taking the big trophy to show them, Dianna was pulled into a big, loving hug by Grandma Mae who had tears of pride in her eyes.

"I'm so proud of you, Dianna, she said. So proud."

On Sunday, the whole family and Dianna's friends, went to church with Grandma Mae. Dianna wore her pink and green dress, her pearls and cape around her shoulders. She was proud of her team— great diversity superhero/supersheroes in their own right. Amazing diversity change agents on a journey to make a difference for their school by encouraging others to experience different places, people, and perspectives.

She stood bold while she watched her grandmother sing in the choir. She felt committed, determined, and confident about what she needed to do at school to help others recognize that for greatness, our diversity and inclusion must be nourished and nurtured in our communities and organizations.

ACKNOWLEDGEMENTS

This book is a continuation of a personal and professional milestone more than 25 years devoted to advancing human resources and diversity and Inclusion work.

I wish to express my sincere appreciation and gratitude to Michelle Gines, CEO of Purpose Publishing who served as my biggest champion during the pursuit of writing my second book. Her expertise, judgment and support provided the necessary guidance I needed to complete this project.

I would like to extend special things to Natasha Beauchamp, my illustrator. She is a talented, young artist and provided the willingness to share her special talent to assist me in accomplishing my goal.

Finally, I would like to acknowledge all of the young girls like Dianna who are dedicated to projects that make a difference. We must continue to invest in them.

ABOUT THE AUTHOR

Dr. Andrea Hendricks provides strategic vision, inspiration, and focused leadership for the development and implementation of globe diversity, equity and inclusion efforts intersecting with human resources initiatives.

Throughout her career, Dr. Hendricks has been a catalyst for positive change, with a focus on driving programs and services to create shared vision and alignment of DEI strategy with an organization's overall objectives.

A respected, and highly sought-after public speaker, Dr. Hendricks has presented her DEI expertise and thought leadership at conferences, seminars, workshops, and other symposia nationwide.

Hendricks is a graduate of Kansas State University where she earned a Bachelor of Science in Human Development Psychology and Mass Communications and a Master of Science in Student Counseling Psychology and Personnel Services. She also earned a Doctorate in Educational Psychology and Policy Analysis from the University of Missouri-Columbia. Andrea has received a Certificate in Diversity Leadership from the Society of Human Resources Management (SHRM) and Yale University.

She penned her first book entitled, The BIG Journey: Bold Inclusion for Greatness which introduced the Six I's Model of diversity practices. It serves as the foundation and catalyst for inspiring this current book for young readers. Andrea's mission is to share the message of diversity in practical ways for both adults and children. Andrea is married to Terrence Hendricks.

Learn more about Andrea and her other work at:
www.DrAndreaHendricks.com

Connect with Andrea:
www.FaceBook.com/DrAndreaHendricks
Twitter: AndreaHendricks

OTHER WORKS BY THE AUTHOR

The BIG Journey: Bold Inclusion for Greatness
Available in Hardback, Paperback & eBook at www.DrAndreaHendricks.com